HOW TO LOVE A BLACK HOLE

Additional Praise

" . . . Rebecca Fishow's latest book of short fiction, *How to Love a Black Hole*, is a rapid, deft, and illusive collection. Moving between narrational mode with skill and fluidity, these stories explore the domestic, the quotidian, and the intimate within an often surreal, consistently inventive architecture, built out by sharp, surprising prose." —***Chicago Review of Books***

"*How to Love a Black Hole* pulls you into the emotional messiness of life and the importance of our bonds with others, leaving you with an experience that's both heart-wrenching and thought-provoking. The impact of these stories will stay with you, making you reflect on the hidden forces that shape our lives and the complex process of understanding ourselves and those around us." —***MicroLit***

" . . . what sets *How To Love A Black Hole* apart is the sheer strangeness at the heart of most of its stories. Toeing the line between the truly speculative and the merely strange, Fishow fearlessly invokes the odd, the unusual, the paranormal, and the bizarre . . ." —***Necessary Fiction***

Rebecca Fishow

HOW TO LOVE A BLACK HOLE

Conium Press
Portland, OR

How to Love a Black Hole
by Rebecca Fishow

Published in the United States of America

Conium Press
Portland, Oregon
https://coniumpress.com

ISBN 978-1-942387-23-7

Cover design, book editing, and interior layout by James R. Gapinski.
Cover image created by Zhuna and licensed through Shutterstock.

Contents

For Chicken Nugget.

Dr. Ear

Are you kidding, of course I hid it from him, I mean, they say that you're supposed to share everything with your spouse—your menstrual cramps, body count, passwords—but put yourself in my shoes: what would you do, waking with a fleshy, rippled, lump on your lower back that looks like an ear but must be a tumor, so you do, you show your man, of course you do, but his gentle touch makes you wince more in panic than pain as, in his "calm voice," he says it's probably benign, a harmless fluke, but his face is all terror as he tells you a doctor visit never hurts, so the next week at the clinic, there are more ears now, on your arm, your belly, one near your foot, an ear growing off of your original ear, and he sends you a text message every two minutes, with little red hearts, insisting it'll all be okay as you bend forward for this old-man doctor who says, "Looks like ears," and you think, *no shit Sherlock*, and the old guy scowls, so maybe you said it out loud, but either way he sends you to the ear specialist down the hall, who's, if you're being honest, the most immediately lovely doctor, human, you've probably ever met, and he touches your ears gingerly, applies salves, feathers his fingers over every little fold, finds you incredible, you unicorn, you gem, suggests weekly check-ins, and you even tell all this to your husband, who starts pulling every overwhelming trick to make you feel safe, cooking meals, running baths, so careful not to touch your ears, not to hurt or scare you, apologizing, apologizing, when meanwhile you fantasize about Dr. Ear's touch, can't wait for the next time he whispers sweet nothings into each canal, this man who studies, who learns, who knows you, now, like no one has before, and what do you say to your husband when weekly visits turn daily, then there's candlelit dinners, and a weekend tryst, because you're covered now, filthy with ears that Dr. Ear nibbles in a way that melts your soul, so you tell me, how do you say, "Husband, I am finally home"?

When I Was Ten

When I was ten Dad took me to the hospital, convinced there was something wrong with my head. I was nervous, but I trusted he knew what was best for me.

"Little girls don't have the kinds of fears you have, about hunger, the future, and death," he said. "Listen to the doctors, and don't be scared. I'll buy you an ice cream after, if you're good and brave."

A nurse took my hand and led me from the waiting room to an operation theater. This was a teaching hospital, and medical students filled the front-row seats. I lay on the examination table and a surgeon plunged a needle in my arm. That's when I passed out.

When I woke, my attempts at speaking were muffled behind a kind of cage. My upper cranium had been lopped right off and fastened over my face.

"Don't touch," a nurse said when my fingers found their way to my exposed, soft brain. "It'll be difficult, but that's the one part of your body you'll have to keep your hands away from."

When I was eleven, I found a VHS cassette of my operation hidden in the box where Dad kept his secret lover's letters. Since my upper cranium blocked my eyes, as the video played, I could only listen to the surgeon speak through the procedure for his medical students.

"Now I am making the incision. Now I am carefully slicing around her head, easing free the upper cranium. Now I am placing the upper cranium on a sterile metal tray. Write all this down. Nothing here but your average human brain." The last words he spoke, before the video cut out: "This is a perfect example of why we have malpractice insurance."

When I was twelve, Mom took me for my annual doctor's checkup. I sat on the table and tried not to fill my cranium mask with big, nervous tears. As the cold metal stethoscope excited my chest, the doctor said, "Good heartbeat." As the reflex mallet surprised my knee, she said, "A little slow. Have you been touching your *you-know-what*?"

"Never," my mother answered for me, but I don't think the doctor believed her. She lifted the plastic helmet I'd been wearing for protection, and as something cottony pressed and prodded my body shimmered and sparked.

She asked a series of questions to my mom: "Does she sleep well at night? How's her mood? Is she sexually active?"

"What a ridiculous question," my mother said. "We don't discuss lewd topics in our house. I don't appreciate you asking such a thing."

When I was thirteen, a boy from two grades ahead brought me to his father's woodshed. He held my hand, removed my plastic helmet, then I felt him slide his tongue around my exposed brain. My body flashed with a tangle of anger, excitement, and pain.

"Don't be scared," he said, and I tried my best to imagine the boy was handsome. I tried to imagine he was sitting across a booth, lapping at an ice cream cone. He pressed my shoulders to sit me down, and said, "We're just waiting for my friends."

When I was fourteen, a punk rock kid saw my operation online. He waited at my locker and told me I was the most punk rock girl he'd ever seen. At the hardcore shows, we guarded our faces from mosh pit kicks and punches, then I found my courage and together we launched our bodies into the crowd. I kicked. I punched. I danced. I took hits. I felt like I was free.

After one show, we were sweaty and happy. He lit a joint in his car. The smoke swirled around my brain like the steam from a warm bath.

"Do you want to try the tongue-to-brain thing I heard you like to do?" he asked.

I didn't know what to say, so I wrote on my pad of paper, "Do you?"

When I was fifteen, I tried and tried to remove my upper cranium from my face. I pried with pliers and tried to wedge a screwdriver between bone and cheek. Not even the hammer I whacked with made the damn thing budge. Not even the window I placed my head under, before slamming down the pane hard.

When I was sixteen, Dad's secret lover must have been tired of being a secret. She posted a video online, then sent the link to my mom. I listened to Dad and the other woman bouncing and writhing on the bed. After it was over, I heard something heavy crash near Dad in the dining room.

"She isn't even pretty," Mom said. "She isn't as pretty as me."

Dad stumbled into the living room and collapsed onto the couch next to me. I imagined he held his head low between his legs. "I don't love her for her looks," he moaned. "I love her for her brain."

When I was seventeen, to help Mom pay the bills after Dad moved out, I got a weekend job as a masseur's apprentice, downtown. I cleaned the massage tables, washed the towels, lit scented candles, and chose calm, quiet music. I worked so well that the masseuse asked me to be her second set of hands.

"I can't see," I wrote to the masseuse. "How will I know where to touch?"

"You don't need your eyes," she said. "You only need to feel."

Now that I am eighteen, I am mostly home alone. Mom works double shifts at a nursing home, taking care of almost-dead people. The neighborhood is quiet, but I lock the door anyway, just in case. One night, I lay in bed, but couldn't fall asleep. I let my fingers feather up my body towards my head, and I couldn't stop myself. I massaged my brain the way I was taught to massage other people's bodies, letting my fingers whisper around the soft mound of flesh, then I gently eased it out. I placed my brain in the shoebox where Dad once kept his secret lover's letters. In the yard, I dug a hole about three feet deep and just wide enough for the box.

Miles

"Where'd you find that?" I asked Ainsley.

When I came home from work, she was sitting at the dining room table studying the journal I'd written during my first pregnancy and kept hidden in a dresser drawer. I managed my feet out of my work flats, paid the babysitter, and sat beside my girl. I'd planned to wait until she was older to tell her, until, perhaps, she was a teenager about to head to college. I didn't want to talk about it now, when she was only eight.

"I never want you to feel like a consolation prize," I said. I slid the book from my daughter's hands and led her to the couch. "He was only two months or so old. He didn't have a torso, like ours. Or a smile, or a temperament, or likes and dislikes. His arms and legs were only itty bitty buds. He was not a son, really. He wasn't even named."

She listened, and I tried to remember what exactly I had

written. I hoped I abandoned the journal before the worst had happened. I hoped I didn't write about the blood in my underwear— dark, and only traces at first before it got much thicker— or the panicked call to the doctor. He'd said I could go to the emergency room if I wanted, but it would just be for peace of mind. I hoped I didn't write about the way I just put on a pad instead and put myself to bed.

I did not tell Ainsley what the near-son did have: a heartbeat that stopped two weeks before my body could let him go. A color picked out for his room. I kept the informal service to myself, and the memorial rock in the yard.

"Weeks later, I became pregnant with you, my little miracle baby."

"Okay," Ainsley said.

"Okay?"

"Okay."

She stood and ran off to play.

After I tucked her in at bedtime that night, I imagined she might never forgive me for lying. I never pretended that Santa Claus or the Easter Bunny was real to avoid that kind of betrayal. I thought of the answers I might give if she started asking existential questions about death or birth. She recently developed a penchant for scaring her little classmates, so I worried about the stories she might tell at school. Would I get a call from her teacher because the other kids were terrified that an undead boy with no face and no fingers was floating through the halls? But after she didn't bring up her almost-brother for a week, I relaxed. Perhaps her child's mind couldn't make the leap from a belly tadpole to the beginnings of a boy. Maybe she had already forgotten, my girl who was still so young that every day gifted her something new.

Then, one night, she tiptoed into my room after I'd gone to bed.

"Mommy," she said, "I met him."

I was groggy. I said, "Met who?"

A boy came to our backyard in Ainsley's dream. He climbed all the way up the treehouse tree, like a little squirrel. He had blond hair, she said, and when he smiled, his freckles stretched across his face like a night sky full of stars. Then he jumped from the top of the tree to the grass and started to play with his toys.

"You were there too, Mommy," she said. "You were sitting in the sun and smiling at him. Was it supposed to be like that?"

I kissed her on the forehead. "It's supposed to be like this."

I came home from work the next day to find my daughter talking to someone in the treehouse. But when I climbed the ladder and peeked through the little door, she was standing by herself. She had her hand flat on the top of her head, then slid out from under it. She hovered her other hand flat in the air.

"Miles is shorter than me," she said. "Girls grow faster

than boys."

"Who's Miles?"

"My brother. My brother Miles."

In the bathtub, she assured me Miles was there. She scrubbed his back with a washcloth and covered his eyes when she poured water on his hair. She began insisting that, before school, I pack two sandwiches, juices, and cookies. On the weekends, she created the *The Miles Book* out of folded construction paper. She filled each page with a Miles fun fact. He was left-handed. He had broken an arm falling from a schoolyard jungle gym. His favorite animal was the tardigrade. His favorite way to travel, a hot air balloon.

My therapist encouraged me not to worry. Children process difficult information in different ways, she said. An imaginary friend was perfectly fine. I don't know why I could not tell him that as my daughter played with Miles, my near-son was a cluster of cells unraveling in my brain, a perpetual letting of blood and flesh. I don't know why I could not tell him I was lowering his body into the ground on repeat.

"Read us a story," she said.

So, I read.

"Buy that shirt for Miles."

I bought.

"Kiss Miles goodnight, too!"

I puckered my lips and kissed the air she promised was

his forehead.

For a week, I couldn't get comfortable in bed or fall asleep. When I couldn't stand the tossing and turning anymore, the staring at the wall, I got myself up. I turned on a little lamp in the kitchen, searched the refrigerator, and sat in the dark dipping my fingers into a peanut butter jar and licking them one by one. I put my feet up on a chair. I listened to appliances buzz.

Freckles bright as stars across his face. Blond hair and a scar on his arm from a playground fall. Bright green eyes. Short, yes. A tiny boy. He didn't look much like my daughter, but yes, they were certainly siblings. Who has been cooking your meals, all this time? Who has been brushing your teeth?

He walked toward me from the doorframe and stood close. He reached and touched my hair. He held his hands around my head and guided my ear to his chest.

Miles. Miles. Miles, it pulsed.

"Feel," he said.

I did.

Haunts

Bedroom: Wake in a bed composed of him, your cheek pressed into the downy lanugo padding on his skin, your skull tucked gently into the whorl of his ear. Keep your fingers suctioned inside the wet cave of his mouth. Curl your limbs around the softness of his gut. Let his breathing roll you like a lifeboat lost at sea. Pull his plump pink arms across your empty torso. Ignore the alarm clock. Let his coos and gurgles ripple like a cat's purr through your dreams.

Office: He hovers weightless over your desk, self-contained and glowing like a lamp too dim for productivity, and just bright enough to keep you awake. His light pulses but never grows. When you open your laptop it smells of soap, milk, bread. When you drag the mouse across the desk, his eyes widen into coins. Your to-do list is a pile of ashes, a thin ribbon of sage. What is a paper clip? What is a power cord? He reaches for these objects, but you won't let him play. The marks you manage are the script of a language you have invented but cannot read.

Kitchen: Perform your banishing spells. Measure. Chop. Stir. Dice. Kneed. Keep busy. Carve. Bake. Hover around warm objects and anoint yourself with thyme. Flip page after page of cookbook after cookbook. If the bread sprouts fungus, if fruit flies make their rounds. If the milk sours, keep going. Cook for your elderly parents and for your neighbors. Carry offerings door to door. Leave muffins on park benches for strangers. Fill decorative fountains with soup. Cover all tables. Stock the pantry. Fill the freezer. Do not look out the window where he may appear in brief, but brilliant flashes. Where he may appear in the form of clouds, or leaves, or street signs. Do not ask about his appetite or wonder about his hunger. Whisk. Crush. Mince. Dissolve. Scramble. Simmer. Stew.

Bathroom: The water is not his blood. The water is not his tears. The pipes do not pump his insides out. The water is not amniotic fluid. The water is not his saliva. The water is not his urine or sweat. The water is nothing holy, nothing baptismal. It is not sperm, nor egg. The water is just water. It makes no promises of keeping you clean.

Attic: How many maybes have you stored in this attic? How many mazes have been built between boxes? How many spiders and how many urns? How many unboxed thoughts? How high can you stack new and ancient stings? If you can part with one whisper, can you part with them all? How long can you lay on dusty wood floors and handle the stagnant heat? How many options? How many ghosts.

Backyard: You have your body. You have the air and the breeze. You can close your eyes, you can listen. Bees buzz in the clover patch. Mosquitos suck your blood. So many birds with their twirls of song, their batting wings carrying all their weight. A million leaves forever flutter on tree limbs. Sunlight blasts its way through even tightly clenched lids. Light fills any space. Your skin is here to absorb heat. If your body isn't a vessel, it may be a blanket. Through a neighbor's open window, a baby cries. Only just waking up.

Forever Overhead

After he brings himself to say yes and has relaxed a bit at the wedding reception, his fourth wife tosses the bouquet over her shoulder, but the hydrangea, thistle, and forget-me-nots hover above the bachelorettes' heads, refusing to come down. In attempts to appease the shrieking women, his new wife promises to hand-deliver each their own bouquet, post honeymoon. The male guests go into problem-solving mode. They discuss the physics of levitation and throw forks toward the sky. The forks, like the flowers, remain in the air, high above the party's heads.

"No matter," the husband says. He waves off the event manager, who has returned from a broom closet with a ladder. The husband announces this is probably a good sign that their love will never fall.

The drive to the secluded honeymoon resort winds along the cliffs of a craggy coast. The newlyweds unpack and then have sex in a bedroom full of soft, expensive things. Beyond their windows, waves batter the rocks, and the seamless ocean rolls on with irritating monotony.

On the beach, his new wife stretches across a lounge chair. Her gold jewelry, emerald string bikini, and long, toned legs make her look regal. She sips a margarita and reads a book while he goes for a long swim.

By the time storm clouds roll in, they are asleep on beach towels, having their individual dreams. They wake to a blanket of raindrops suspended above their heads.

"Another good omen," the husband insists to his fourth wife. When she shivers, he reassures her with a forehead kiss.

The parasailing incident worries him, though. They are out to sea on a small speedboat and when it's time to lower his wife back down, no matter how hard the operator tugs on the winch, he can't get her to move. She stays overhead, kicks her legs, and laughs and screams at once.

"She may come down on her own if we cut the rope," the operator says.

"We'll figure it out," says the helmsman, then he starts the engine and steers the men away and back towards the shore.

The next day, lounge chairs, patio tables, sun umbrellas, and beach balls levitate over the cabana bar and pool. The activities manager finds the husband there, floating face-up in the water.

"She must have wandered off," he says and admits that

when the crew returned to the scene, the man's wife was simply gone. He reminds the husband of the liability waver he signed before the excursion, then offers him vouchers and resort merchandise, but the gifts float away from their hands.

Back home, the husband crumples wedding cards and wrapping paper into balls. He pitches them toward the waste basket where they hover in the air and refuse to fall. The cat leaps at a fly and gets stuck with its legs spread wide and its tail puffed up. The air in the condo grows thick with hairs, skin flakes, and stray fibers. Outside, each day, the sky fills with a little more clutter. Basketballs, garden hoses, abandoned kid shoes. Blades of mown lawn and litter. It seems to the man he is living, now, in a world that exists mostly above him.

For a moment, he mistakes a woman floating over the grocery store parking lot, her arms loaded with shopping bags, her hair wild and long, for his lost fourth wife. After that, he finds himself looking vaguely for her in the sky. Downtown, a woman who is not his wife hovers drunk above a bar. Another levitates in a jumping pose beside a freeway bridge. He lets his beard grow out, lets the housekeeper go. He lets his desk stay empty at work.

He drives hours north to a mountain range, buys a ticket for a cog railroad train, and rides it up to the highest peak. Conifers give way to squat bushes, then a landscape of rock and lichen. The winds kick up, the temperature drops, and the sky grows full of clouds. On the summit, he separates himself from the tourists and finds an isolated ledge. With a blanket of peaks stretching out below him, he reaches his arms above his head and draws himself up on his toes. A little girl in a pink ski suit waves his way as she floats across his view.

Let's have a baby, he thinks, when he is back in his seat, the train is chugging down the mountain. It was something he must have said long ago, or a line from a conversation he never actually had but thought he one day might. It was a sentence, perhaps, he overheard in a park from what felt like a comfortable distance.

Open Up

Darcy opens up her legs for her ex-boyfriend. She's on her back, on a picnic table, on a private beach between the Hudson River and an impossible limestone mansion. She's ignoring the pains shooting through her stomach and up her throat. The way her ex fucks might be laughable to another kind of person. He goes at her like a vulture shredding a scavenged animal. *Thrust-thrust-thrust*, but it works for Darcy. She usually feels like roadkill.

The mansion condo that belongs to Darcy's great aunt is full of expensive furniture and paintings that could make an auctioneer sing. It's full, too, of her great uncle's things: shirts and files and books that have no purpose anymore, except to remind her great aunt of her husband's absence. It's late, and Darcy hopes the condo lights stay dark.

There's a scar on her forehead, a memory knocked in, a gift from her ex's bedroom dormer that time they were screwing on his desk, back at college. This is a kind of passion, a kind of love. Medicine, even, for the right person. He has chicken legs, and he's shorter than Darcy, but he's powerful when he's fucking. He's a textbook only child, eager for praise. On the picnic table, he rolls Darcy to her stomach and he's off to the races. Her breasts smash flat and her thighs sear against the table ledge. In Darcy's sight: the pristine mansion at the end of a multi-tiered lawn adorned with stone patios and imported flora that remind her of the bourgeoisie.

Her great aunt's husband was buried last fall, and a month after that, the woman's femur snapped on a stair. Weeks ago, when Darcy arrived for the summer, she was surprised by the withered iteration of her great aunt that met her at the door. Darcy hadn't seen her in years, but she remembered her elegant and serene. Now the black dress was colossal on her whittled frame. Her voice shook when she spoke to Darcy, and her cheeks looked puffy and sagged.

Darcy's ex yanks a fistful of hair, but the posture is too technical, so he clutches her shoulder instead. He's not a bad person. Darcy knows he's good. But his sexual diet's all Hollywood and porn.

"This is hot," he says between low moans. "I've never done it outside or in public."

Darcy is an old hat at the risky sex game. She's screwed on rooftops and bathroom stalls. On forest floors and in moving cars. She's gotten men off under tables, in movie theaters. They found her exciting at first.

Everything about the summer has been painful, but Darcy keeps the reasons to herself. An eating disorder that just won't quit. The hideaway bed that must be a half-century old jabbing her with its coils. She stopped unfolding it, and now she's sleeping on the floor. She wakes up sore and twisted, but she's afraid to make a fuss. She is supposed to be making her great aunt's life easier, but Darcy can't even do that for herself. Her eating problems are harder to deal with here, and the anxiety attacks feel like dying. She can't afford next semester's tuition, so she replaced her New York City internship with a hostessing job two miles down the road.

"Young people," the great aunt has said. "You're so busy nowadays."

Darcy wishes her ex would hurry and finish, go back to his place in Jersey so she can be alone with the river. He ramps up, pulls out, comes on her back, and she lets her muscles relax. She has to ease her thighs off the table slowly to minimize the pain.

"Give me a minute," the show-off says. He rubs himself and gears up for round two. Darcy thinks about the way, when she visited this place as a child, her great aunt's mornings always looked the same. A newspaper read slowly to the soundtrack of quiet classical music. Yorkshire tea sipped from an artisan mug, and a view of the river through wide, clean windows. Her husband sitting next to her, reading the paper, too. Now it's just the great aunt in the living room, and Darcy tiptoeing past the door on the way to the kitchen, hoping she won't hear.

Her great aunt has been making almost no progress vanishing the presence of her husband from the house. When Darcy gets back from her late restaurant shifts, not even a pair of his reading glasses has been boxed. None of his files have been thrown out.

One day, last week, the old woman said she wanted to talk. Darcy sat across from her at the kitchen table staring at her hands. She was already anxious and feeling disgusting. At work, she hadn't been able to stop releasing gas. It happens sometimes, she gets so constipated that she bloats right up and has no choice. Her boss walked to the hostess booth where Darcy stood for hours every evening. "What is that? It smells like rotten eggs over here," he said, then covered his mouth and gagged.

"I thought you would be helping me a little more," her great aunt said at the table, "but you're so busy, and when you're here, you're so quiet that I don't feel like I can ask."

"I want to help. Tell me what you need, and I'll do it."

Their eyes began to well with tears, and they both tried not to cry.

When he's hard again, Darcy's ex positions her to face the river. One foot on the picnic table bench adds traction for his favorite trick. It hurts when he goes for her ass, and makes

Darcy's body clench up, but she's not all that bothered by the pain. Her body is a tired adversary, and she secretly hopes all this pounding will stimulate her bowels. As he's going at it, her new view is really beautiful. The distant hills. The river lapping the shore. The gently fading stars. Cars rolling over the Tappan Zee bridge, going anywhere away.

When the relationship ended, she knew she had broken his heart. "I love you! I love you! I love you!" he said, like he was desperate to convince them both. Darcy could tell that he finally understood what was true from the beginning: She wouldn't be able to recognize love if it was screwing her in the ass.

He spares Darcy's back this time and orgasms into the sand. He makes a college try of eking an orgasm out of her, but it's useless, and she doesn't try to fake it. They sit and hold hands for a couple of minutes, but there's nothing much to say. They know how this is going to end. Up the hill, inside the mansion, her great aunt will wake up soon, and Darcy feels guilty about everything she is.

As she holds his hand and watches the water throb against the little beach, Darcy imagines her great aunt at her age, sitting at this picnic table. In her imagination, the young woman wears a sundress, a wide straw hat, and big sunglasses like a cinema starlet. She sees her aunt waving to her brand-new husband as he paddles his strong arms against the current. Their entire life is ahead of them, and though his long strokes carry him further from land, she's certain he will return.

Go Back

Before the two-month stints in Djibouti. Before the machine guns and the all-hours shifts. The flies blacking out the sky and the blackouts. Go back before the defense contract salary paid for your houses, your nightmares, your long list of deathdays. Forget the muscly Trump flag over your temporary bed. The sandstorms. The beheadings. The suicide bombs. Al-Shabaab. Go back before Poland and spying on Russian spies. The code names. Your intel. The checkpoints. The scans. The close calls have not occurred. You're back before drinking on leave becomes your best life. Before hangover headaches. Raw throats and toilet bowls. Before mimosas for breakfast and cocktails at lunch.

Go back to orange soda. Hot dogs grilled juicy and slathered with ketchup, before ketchup resembled spilled blood. Replace the bodies with buns. Before that time, during an interrogation, that a sergeant made you impersonate an Iraqi woman to get an assassin to talk. Before tracking dots on 3-D maps and alerting higher-ups when they crossed the wrong lines. Go back before the higher-ups alerted the ground troops and the ground troops killed the dots.

Remember how I hated mayonnaise on burgers? Remember the orange soda we never got to have, except on days like this? Mown lawn and butter and sun-warmed tar. When the Fourth of July meant sprinklers and pools. Remember fireworks and fireflies. Forget explosives and fires. Before detached limbs and scorched skin there were ribs and fingers and wings.

Your fellow Marines' limbs never scattered like litter across the dirt.

Remember leaping from swings. Forget diving from planes. Forget the casualty reports you composed: your first MOS. Before a Humvee drill at Camp Pendleton flattened your friend. Forget the gas chamber burning your lungs at Parris Island. The sexism in barracks and mess halls. Those horny, barely legal, male Marines who clutched at your flesh and called you slut.

Forget, at eighteen, that Marine recruiter who rolled his eyes and scoffed, "Why would you want to join those Air Force pussies? Marines are the toughest there is." Forget all those acronyms. WMD. IED. MOS. MRE. The surgeries that fixed your legs after combat training broke them. The time you told me you were shipping out again because they need more "bodies" in Iraq. Before the flashbacks there were watermelon slices. Pink dripping down your chin. Before the anger there were the summers we gorged on macaroni salad and drank so much orange soda our tongues stayed stained. Go back to the time we were simply sisters playing Teenage Mutant Ninja Turtles. You, the blue ninja every damned time. The toughest fighter, the leader of the pack. Me, April O'Neil, ready to report. The only thing you killed were the nemeses of our imaginations. The only things marching were the armies of ants, and all they wanted was sugar in the sun.

Tornado Warnings

Here there are tornado warnings every other day. The winds pick up and the leaves spiral tightly around themselves. Shingles threaten to snap from the walls of the old family home. Every other day, she wonders which version of her husband she will receive and which version of herself will be there to receive him. They only speak to each other, now, through a taut string between tin cans.

On days when there are tornado warnings, she likes laying open-faced in the yard watching the sky for signs of violence. The tin-can phone carries her concerns into the house to her husband as unpredictably as the weather. Sometimes, tornados speed through and snap the cans away, slapping the string into spindly pieces. Sometimes his replies come through muddled and all torn up. Once in a while, her husband isn't on the other side at all, and she wonders who she is speaking to so urgently.

The yard is full of dead leaves, insects, and flower petals. She rakes cricket torsos and dandelion puffs into a pile and says a prayer for the dead. The funny thing about tornado warnings: they are only warnings, not promises or truths. Still, she is so fearful, and feels so small, that there's hardly a difference between a warning and the real thing.

First the tornado warning, then she discovers the version of her husband she gets that day. Today, in the kitchen, he floats over the dirty dishes and counter crumbs. He flails his arms and shouts profanities through the cans. This version of her husband is zipped over several others: a layer of hunger over a layer of horniness over a layer of exhaustion. She knows to keep her distance until he floats out the door for work.

Instead of entering the kitchen to try and comfort him, she climbs the stairs to the one little bedroom with its one little window and one little bed. The version of him thrashing beneath her feet knocks his head on the wall. When he's gone for work, she looks in the mirror in a noncommittal way. She wakes from a nap as a monstrous version of herself, all thorns and bunions and puss, then closes her eyes and lets her mind perform furious, spinning tricks. Her husband's side of the bed is a dip that he no longer fills.

According to family mythology, there was once a tornado so powerful but generous that it averted smashing through the home. Instead, it scattered gifts across the yard. Some of the gifts were living: a family dog. A rose bush. A snake. A boy from a village halfway around the world, fleeing a dirty war. Some of the gifts were valuable objects that were divided amongst the children. As the story goes, before the tornado spun away, a cadaver of a rich man smacked down. Its lips were stretched into a smile and its fists were full of rage.

"All right, already," she shouts to the sky. "When will you come? I'm done waiting." She is feeling the same way she sometimes feels driving down the highway when she suddenly remembers she can yank the wheel in either direction and change her life in a flash.

Something Both Terrifying and Comforting

The invitation to the celebration of life said it was a backyard barbecue and potluck. We were welcome to bring a dish or snack. My husband and I were back in New Hampshire, jet-lagged, and Amy said there would be plenty of food already. Still, I wanted to contribute so we stopped at the grocery store on the way to her mother's house. I thought, a veggie platter or tray of sandwiches. No desserts. No shitty bags of chips. I wanted something nourishing that would say, *I will take good care of you during this difficult time. I will keep your body strong.*

The house looked nearly as I'd remembered from childhood, back during the years I'd practically grown up here, the years of sleepovers, study sessions, and blowout fights. Of crafting, first kisses, and prom photos. Of fooling around with strangers, or one another, after unchaperoned parties. Of giving ourselves piercings and bouts of misplaced anger reshaped as self-harm. It looked the same except the slate-blue paint was flaking off the wood.

"Needs a paint job," my husband said as we pulled to the curb. Then, "Are you sure it's okay I'm coming to this? I never met Amy's dad."

"You know Amy. These things are for the living. There they are," I said.

The Santas were shutting their pickup truck doors, ambling towards the backyard, tugging coolers and carrying casserole dishes. Amy's father had been a member of The International Brotherhood of Real Bearded Santas, and here they all were with their cool sunglasses and big white beards, their respectable off-season Santawear. White button-downs and suspenders holding up ironed, red shorts. A few of the Santas slung bright red sport coats over their shoulders, to put on later for the photos.

Out back, Amy stopped hustling to hug me. She didn't have any jobs for me, and she was on a roll placing food on tables and welcoming the guests. Sometimes when people are knee-deep in grief, the best thing to do is hang back and let them keep moving, so my husband headed for the paper plates, and I found the well-stocked bar. I signed the guest book at the memorial table, and it was hard to pull my eyes away from the photographs of Amy's dad projected on a screen, from puffy cheeked child to handyman, to frail and grey old man.

Soon, the other girls arrived, the other half of the fab four, Nia and Jules. Only we weren't girls anymore, and we weren't convinced we were fabulous. We were ambivalent about the fact that we were nearing middle age and trying our best to stay enthusiastic about our lines of work. We lived in different states, and got together once a year, or less. On weekend girls' trips, we allowed ourselves to indulge in questionable quantities of booze and food. We made mild jokes about our jobs and our families, and mostly avoided the difficult topics. Nia's divorce. Amy's lingering, chronic car accident carnage. The various stints of depression and pills. We were the kind of skeptical, childless women who mostly managed to ignore time passing until we were in the presence of one another's new wrinkles. Or, until one of our parents got sick and died.

When I told my father that Amy's dad was terminal, he asked, "How old was he?" seeking clues.

The Santas and Mrs. Clauses set up their lawn chairs in a wide circle at the far end of the yard. They looked cozy and jolly, lounging with their heaps of food and summer ales in Koozies.

Amy joined us after she finally ran out of tasks and had finished making her rounds.

"I'm going to be a mess come Christmas time," she said.

"I'll distract you with Hanukkah," I offered, but a Mrs. Claus came around with a basket of jingle bells. The cards tied to the little velvet bags read in elegant cursive, next to a photo of her Santa dad, *Believe and I will be there!*

There weren't any distractions after that.

Except, we hoped, the lake.

After the party, the girls and I drove two hours to Nia's newly purchased cabin on the tiny lake in the empty middle of Maine. My husband came too, just this one time. The cabin was surrounded by forest and built right next to the shore. We opened all the window shutters and chose beds, then settled in the sun, on the deck.

"This is my first real vacation since I don't know how long," Amy said. She looked out at the water from her Adirondack chair. "All my travel has been coming back home to help with Dad."

So, we tried to make it as vacationy as possible. We hooked up the speaker, made mimosas, lay our beach towels on the dock. We pushed through the water on flamingo and narwhal floats. We broke out more booze and took turns trying to balance on Nia's paddle board. We dubbed my husband an honorary girl, but didn't wake him when he passed out on the couch, and enjoyed the time to ourselves.

"I need food," he said when he woke, and we were suddenly all ravenous. Amy unpacked a cooler of leftovers from the celebration of life, and we stuffed ourselves with barbecue ribs, pasta salads, and loaded mushrooms. We went in for seconds and brought the plates around to the campfire pit, where we were happy to let my husband fall into the role of stoker.

Amy told stories about her father's last night, how she'd been the one to find him unbreathing in his favorite reclining chair. After the ambulance left, her mother said, "Time to break out the booze," then they drank at the dining room table through the night. She crossed the street in a rainstorm to bum a cigarette from a neighbor and pet his dog

In the last bits of sunlight, the loons started up. Their deep, solitary cries echoed across the lake.

"I read that loons have four distinct calls," Amy said. "One means, 'Hey! Where are you guys?' Another means, 'Want to fuck?'"

"Did you know the loon call is the most common sound used in horror and sci-fi movies to convey dread and terror," said Nia, our film connoisseur. "It makes ornithologists crazy because they use the sound in parts of the world where loons don't even live."

"I think it's a comforting sound," I said. "It always made me feel calm."

My husband asked, "What do the other sounds mean?" but none of us had the answer.

The fire died down past midnight. After we all said goodnight my husband and I climbed the ladder to the guest bed in the loft. I tried my best to make my thoughts turn off by whispering a loon call.

"Are you saying, 'want to fuck?'" my husband asked. He was falling asleep, and I laughed. But it felt more like, "Where are you?" to me. Or one of the calls we didn't understand. Something both terrifying and comforting. I closed my eyes, took my husband's hand, and thought of Amy downstairs, in a bedroom by herself. I imagined her trying to believe deeply enough to bring her father back.

When We Shrunk

When we shrunk, I took your tiny hand and squeezed it so hard in my tiny hand that you must have known I loved you. When we shrunk, we made swimming pools of our coffee cups, held our noses, and jumped. We climbed the stairs to the bedroom with belay ropes you crafted out of dental floss. When the whole world ballooned around us, bigger than I cared to imagine, bigger than made sense, we made ourselves fit.

I looked into your eyes and said, "Right-sized." I ran my hand up your leg and said, "My size." Cars had never been so frightening before. Doorways had never been entrances to temples. Insects had never been horses. We could have played that tired game of whose fault is this? We could have done a lot of crying.

When we shrunk, we exchanged other questions: How do we deal with the tumbleweeds of dust? These stray hairs that could be lassos or nooses. What work is worth it? Who, out there, will notice us now? We bought an apple, a single chicken thigh. One baby carrot lasted for a month. We had never said grace before, but we made our hands into pairs of arrows. I thanked the enormous world for what I no longer needed. You thanked it for the change.

When we shrunk, at least we were still alive. We didn't disappear yet, like our grandparents, then our parents, one after another. Like the massive cat we could have ridden like royalty, room to room. Like the tree disappeared, and the shoreline. Like one star after another. When you were in another room, I got scared and called, "Are you there?"

"In here," you said.

"In where?"

You spent a weekend wandering under the bed. The closet became your mountain range. You scaled the apartment walls towards the sills, as strong and agile as ever. You threw an arm over the ledge and looked out all the windows.

"Come up," you said, "Look how big."

What more could you have needed than this too-big place? How could I have tried to stop you? There was your still-large brain full of all its wants. There was an open window. I imagined you smaller than an atom. Smaller than a quark. I imagined you so small I wouldn't miss you when you leaped.

High School Mixtape

Side 1: He was always a freak / He never tried to fit in / He head-butted his rival / He wrote a story about a serial killer / I saw him shoot a squirrel with a bb gun in second grade / He ate lunch in the bathroom / He drew a swastika on the cafeteria wall / His father was in jail / His mother waited tables at the strip joint / He threatened to beat the shit out of some kid who called him fat / He listened to death metal / He was on the spectrum, or something / He had an eating disorder, or something / He was a certified schizophrenic / It was like one day a switch just flipped / They should have seen it coming / He liked the dark side of the Web / He never had a girlfriend / He failed all his classes / So many red flags / He worked at the shooting range / He wore all black and had neck tattoos / He said he wanted to be dead when he grows up / He carried around a weird black notebook / He mapped it all out on his

Twitter feed / He never spoke in class / He slept in class / He laughed for no reason / He liked to cut class / He got sent to the principal's office for threatening to filet the teacher. They gave him a warning, told him to shape up, then they sent him back him right back to class.

Side 2: He's such a freak / Nobody likes him / I heard the lacrosse players used to kick his ass every day / He wrote this gay story about his dog that died / During recess, he talks to a squirrel like a friend / He is definitely not sitting at our table / He got major offended by the swastika on the lunch room wall / I think his father's in jail / I heard his mother fucked the principal, his sister too / He's big as a planet / He listens to shit music / He's retarded, or something / He's on the three-finger diet / That kid is definitely hearing voices / It's like, one day he was semi-normal, and now he's whatever / He totally looks like a school shooter / He's in the dumb-people classes / So many red flags / He's on welfare, I think / He wears too-small clothes that smell like a dumpster / He said he wants to be more himself when he grows up / He carries around this weird black notebook / He trolls all the popular kids on Twitter / He looks like he's going to cry like a baby whenever the teacher calls on him / He farts in class / He got held back a year / He got me sent to the principal's office, ratted me out, then my boys went and found him after class.

The Shamash

Rivka's sister, Shira, is twenty-seven and somewhere upstate. On the other side of the gate, the warden and a guard are treating her like a sideshow act: gawking and whispering, wary, but curious. She feels their eyes linger on her prison pounds, her softened, dimpled arms, her salt-swollen face. She is beyond communication with men like these, and when the warden passes her last meal tray through the steel bars, she keeps her eyes fixed on the concrete floor.

"Potato pancakes. Enjoy," the warden says, and there's no need to correct him, no need to say *latkes*. She sits on the chair in the furthest corner of the cell and whispers a private prayer.

Barukh ata Adonai Eloheinu melekh ha'olam…

With a plastic spork she scrapes sour cream and apple sauce from condiment cups, smears them on the latkes, and cuts a thick slice. A quilt of oil, onion, and potato wraps her backfiring brain and she's gone. The guard says something, but she does not hear. She's years away, age seven, on the last night of Hanukkah, absorbed in the menorah's flickering lights, reminders of God's grace. Another bite, and she is age nine again, playing "Who Can Eat Most?" at the table with Rivka, stuffing latkes through her lips as fast as she possibly can. Her mouth is a flood of saliva and salt, but Rivka, with her boundless hunger, always wins the game.

Each bite of latke tastes of flesh and sweat. Of blood, semen, and amniotic fluid. Shira chews and she is fifteen again, staring at her body in the full-length bedroom mirror. She slides down her pajama pants to examine her widening hips and womanly gut. She peels off her nightshirt, and the sight of her newly grown breasts produces ripples of pleasure and fear. Then she twists her arm to inspect the purple blooms of her father's fingers bruised in.

Before school, Shira and Rivka work heavy stockings to their waists. They fasten wool skirts and button long-sleeved blouses. In the kitchen, their mother is wigged and proper as she fills a platter with leftover latkes, then eats across from the girls, while, under the table, Rivka passes Shira a folded note. Shira unfolds and flattens on her lap it as quietly as she can. She forces a starchy swallow as she reads: *Baby. Gentile. Secret.*

In Jewish culture, a saying: Jews don't have history, they have memory. History is learned. Memory, felt. History is the bars, the warden, the concrete cell, all dissolving as Shira chews. She chews, and she's twelve years old, at shul, the day she realizes what the prayer really means. While the men's morning blessing thanks God they were not made female, women thank God for making them in his image. She bites, and she's her mother, now, following tzniut, forbidden to sing before her father, forbidden to show her hair. She chews, and she's her sister, Rivka, curled and shaking on the floor of a bathroom stall at school. Next to her, the pregnancy test floats in the toilet bowl. Shira licks sour cream from the corner of her mouth, and is herself again, holding Rivka's hair, a week later, same bathroom. A bite and she sneaks off to the pharmacy, pockets prenatal pills.

She's Hagar, beaten by Sarah while pregnant, banished to the woods. A bite and she's Esther in the king's Harem, a part of his property. A bite and she's Gomer in front of her jealous husband, who threatens to thrust her, naked, upon men who will rape and beat. She pushes two whole latkes into her mouth, lets them stuff her cheeks. She's Rivka, seventeen, six months pregnant and showing, cowering on the living room floor. Their father's fists pound down upon her rounded back. She's herself, Shira, twisted with wrath, the brass menorah clutched and raised in her hands, then thrust down on her father's skull.

God's words, she hears: *Thou shalt not kill. But, if a thief is found at home, and beaten to death, no sin.*

The warden paces, and whispers to the guard.

"Finished?" he says, but she doesn't set down her plate. She is somewhere else, somewhere holy.

Somewhere, Rivka is alive with her child, cooking latkes in boiling oil. A bite and she's her niece savoring the oil, onions, and salt. She's her niece unable to gaze away from the miracle candle light.

"Thieves," she says when the guard tries to tug the empty plate from her hands.

She is Judas, a warrior erecting an altar of unhewn stones. She is sturdy, alight, pulsing, and wild. Wailing, full, and electric. The temple of her body will not be dismantled. She smashes the plate to the ground.

Notes From the Harvest

Springtime, I mother a scab until it bleeds into a bowl. The cat laps the blood until her mouth turns red. In the kitchen, my mother hacks her mother into tiny pieces. I sneak a pie off the counter, up the stairs, and into the bedroom. My husband and I eat it all.

We bury my grandmother in the front garden as the neighbors surround us and sing funeral hymns. My mother lies on the repacked dirt, moans, and bathes in moonlight. My husband and I join the neighbors around her, humming and holding hands. He shutters a little, and his foot tap-tap-taps. He cracks his knuckles twice.

"I want this for you," I tell my husband, "If you need to go, then you should." He is not from around here and will leave again soon. We don't know if he'll return.

Late summer, my grandmother sprouts along with the rest of the neighborhood dead. Just a finger at first. Then an ear and a heel. A hand bursts out of the soil. Her toes bloom from her feet like cactus flowers, and her breasts spread like soft moss mounds. We know that each year if we water her right, she will return.

As tradition dictates, my mother allows the neighborhood children to harvest our yield. My husband is gone now, but if he was here, the sight of the young ones reaping their bounty would have reminded him of his favorite possible future. "Are you ready to have kids of your own?" he has asked more than once, and each time I deflected. "I wonder why the cat loves blood," I said. "I wonder why we love pies, and why children love plucking the dead."

Because we are no secret, my hometown lover and I leave my bed, dress to join hands and sing with the neighbors in the garden of a man who has died. "I'll pick you one of his arms when he blooms," my hometown lover says, and I wish he was my husband. I wonder what kind of rituals exist wherever he is now.

The cat likes the gardens as much as the children and my lover. She rubs her coat against exposed wrists, claws thighs, and nibbles nails. My lover harvests a bicep. I moonbathe when I'm alone.

Come winter, the holiday market's full swing in the parking lot of the local dive bar. My man and I drink until we're swaying, then buy a pie as big as the moon at a baked goods stall outside. He buys a bushel of decorative tongues. Because he is a sloppy drunk, he knocks over a table of soft, curly hair. I think about what he doesn't know as he scrambles to gather it up: tonight, I will not let him home with me; I will sneak the pie past my mother, who sleeps, now, in the garden, waiting for her turn; when I've finished the pie, I'll pick this scab again and the blood will beckon the cat; I'll think, again, that if I keep this up, it's surely going to scar.

Cockroaches

"Cockroaches," she tells him, "are my biggest fear."

"Cockroaches?" he asks. He is not her husband. He's just a man.

"When I was little," she says, "my dad worked as a delivery driver for his brother, who owned a textile business in the sketchiest part of town. One day, he lets me tag along in the truck, and when we're done with deliveries, he takes me back to explore the factory. Inside, I have to go to the bathroom all of a sudden, really, really bad. So, Dad gives me a flashlight to maneuver through the winding halls. When I finally find a bathroom, I rush into a stall and sit. *Yes, such a relief.* I'm about to wipe when suddenly I feel a tickling sensation on my ass. I use the flashlight to investigate, and hundreds of cockroaches come scuttling from the toilet. There are so many they start covering my shit, the bowl, my ass. I feel them making their way down my legs and they start dropping to the floor. I didn't even get a chance to pull up my pants. I jumped up and ran out fast as hell."

"Cockroaches," the man who is not her husband mutters. His cheeks inflate like he might puke.

"Cockroaches all the way down," she says.

He slithers off his bar stool and scuttles back to the corner booth from whence he came just as the man who is her husband flicks his butt outside the window and joins her at the bar.

"Cockroaches?" he asks.

"Works every time."

Except, she thinks, as he orders his drink, *it didn't work with you.* He's late, and he smells like another woman's cloying, cheap perfume.

Once, her husband filled the toilet with stupid plastic cockroaches. Once, he laughed when she screamed at a cockroach darting down a hall. What if he sneaks a cockroach into her hair or slips one into her purse? What if a cockroach scampered into his pant leg as he was putting them back on, and now it's about to make its way from his body to hers?

He waits for his drink, catches her looking toward the corner, and glances pensively at the man.

"Did I ever tell you *my* greatest fear?" he asks. "How about you guess?"

She guesses dying alone. Dementia and heights. She

guesses the ocean and public speaking. She guesses being murdered by an angry woman, being chopped up and stuffed in a wall.

"Cockroaches?" she guesses, but he doesn't laugh. His hand on her thigh feels clenched.

"Monotony," he says, and sips his beer.

The man who is not her husband settles up. "Watch out for those cockroaches, Sweetie, they'll get you," he says with some cheer as he passes.

She gives a quick wink, without thinking.

At home, she tells her husband she is going up to sleep. She's drunk enough to do it. She dreams she can survive a nuclear blast and live without her head. She dreams her eyes have thousands of lenses, and she can see everything wriggling her way.

If She Finds You

Like you've imagined she would, if she cuts the engine in front of the sun-scorched lawn, you might watch her through the mini blinds as your heart icepicks at your ribs. You might wait by the door as she breathes in her car, closes her eyes, tries to calm her hands. She might smooth her skirt in a compulsive way that also belongs to you.

If she makes it to the front door, you could choose to be home, let her in, or not. Throw your arms around her, let your fingers comb her hair. If she has sat with her parents, requested records, tracked you down, you can say you've imagined this day all her life, then study the changes in her facial expression when she gets a good look at your place.

Piles of old papers, tangled cords in heaps. Trash bags stuffed with old clothes. Worn shoes and takeout containers stacked on the table. Broken lamps and boxes of empty pill bottles you cannot throw away. You are organizing, you might say. Getting ready to donate. Or she caught you unpacking from a move. As you clear the couch of its heaps of junk, you could try to convince her it's all just inventory for the thrift store where you work.

If she's finally really and truly here, cross-legged and quiet on your couch, you can scrounge up the photo album hidden in the back of the closet. Here is the hospital bed holding both of your bodies. Here are her inky, tiny footprints, a lock of her hair. Here is a photo of the bassinet you assembled during a moment of foolish hope.

You could unbury a sleeve of paper cups and offer to make her coffee. You have creamer, but it's months expired, and there's no oat milk, no artificial sweetener, no fancy fixings you imagine she prefers. You've always imagined she's lived the affluent childhood that you couldn't offer. It's too painful to consider the possibility she's been as bad off, or worse.

As she talks, you can locate the parts of her that do not come from you and certainly not from him. The Burberry coat folded neatly in her lap. A pair of pearl stud earrings and modest leather flats. Her SAT vocabulary sounds natural on her lips, and her ballerina posture must have come from years of classes. You can try not to worry about what she thinks of your Walmart sweatshirt or your drugstore dye job. You can feel relief or fear, or simply something like love. You can divulge, deny, or deflect.

When she leaves, you might resolve to make progress for real this time: Throw away the piles of clothes and the useless cords, scrub the dirt from the floor. Despite this progress, you could allow yourself to pocket her used tissue. Keep her paper cup and kiss the champagne-pink lipstick smudge.

You may be too ashamed, after all, to let her enter the house. Instead, if she calls, you might make plans to meet her at the Applebee's in the strip mall. This way, you can choose to be somebody else altogether. A lawyer, a librarian, a private school teacher. Before catching the bus, you can rummage through the top dresser drawer and find your mother's cubic zirconia necklace. You could dig out the straightening iron, try to tame your frizzy hair.

While she parks her sensible Audi that you imagine she got as a sweet sixteen gift, you can ask the hostess to seat you at a corner booth. There, the dim lighting may hide the circles around your eyes and any of her features that might remind you of him, like his square jaw, high hairline, or deceptively kind eyes. As she tells you about her high school experience, her hobbies, and her likes, you might choose to identify the parts of her that definitely came from you. Her soft, ridged fingernails, her gently hooked nose. Her slight, anxious stutter and pensive pauses. She might have your laugh, your eyebrows, and your nervous blink, but her smile might be all fucking his. Order the shrimp and parmesan sirloin, the most expensive item on the menu. Encourage her to choose any food she wants. "Let me spoil you," say. "Tell me everything."

Maybe she'll have two younger brothers, adopted like her. Maybe her bedroom's baby blue, and her favorite book is *The Red Tent*. If she says she has applied to a couple of ivies but isn't holding her breath, tell her, "Of course they'll accept you. How can they not?" Because how could anyone else reject her after what you did?

If she finds you, and you meet her at Applebee's, you can unclasp your mother's necklace from your neck and present it to her as an apology, a promise. When she excuses herself to the bathroom, order Triple Chocolate Meltdown with two spoons. Hope they will let you pay for it all with your EBT card.

It may feel safer to meet somewhere more public. The community garden at the city park, where you've probably both been many times. If she asks about her grandparents, you can tell her just the good. Her grandmother was a gardener, and her father liked to swim. Tell her the name of your college alma mater, but not why you dropped out.

"You have a resting bitch face, just like me," she might say, and it'll make both of you laugh.

If she asks about her father, you bet your ass you can lie. He was a soldier who died bravely in action. A musician traveling through. He was a college professor. An explorer. A prince. Anything, except the truth. The drunken walk home.

The dark sky and abandoned city alley. His body holding yours down. How easily he ignored your punches, your kicks. How surprisingly fast it all was finished.

Most likely, if you're being honest, you won't meet her at all. If she calls or shows up, you'll keep your answers need-to-know. You had her too young. You weren't ready. You had to think about her future. You knew that she deserved so much more than you could give. Hang up. Keep the door locked. Keep the curtains drawn. Sit in your mess in the dark. Try to convince yourself to toughen up and stop dwelling. Stop thinking about how quickly it all was finished, how unfinished a lifeline is.

The Daughters

Edith is our oldest Mommy, her skin nearly translucent. We love watching her warm, blue blood pulse through swollen veins. Roberta has the go of a hopped-up, mid-century housewife. When she gets the zoomies, we give her the vacuum and try to stay out of her way. When she stands on tiptoes to dust the top of the bookshelf, we offer our hands for balance. We let Lucy, our mean Mommy, our yeller and blamer, tell us we're no good. We frown and look down, when she says, "You stupid, ungrateful girls!" But inside, we are jittery with a dozen shades of glee. We're good at our jobs. We age down well with pigtails, bows, ankle socks, Mary Janes. At night, we let our glam mother, Rhonda, smear lipstick across our mouths. She shows us how to bat our eyelashes and how to paint our nails, while Yolanda, our queen-of-love mother, reads us her favorite picture books. We eat her warm cookies two at a time, and before tucking us in for our afternoon naps, Yolanda insists we have one more.

Yes, mommies, we say. Oh, mommies, we need you! We fill the mothers with all our wants, and we always want so much: new dance leotards, a Band-Aid, new jump ropes and skates. We want the night lights on, and we want to stay up late to watch just one more show. We don't care that dinner's in an hour, we're hungry now. We want snacks! We don't want to go read a book when we're bored. We want the mothers to know that they're ruining our lives. We want bikes and a big tree house. We want our siblings to get in trouble, not us. They started it, we say, and point our fingers at one another's faces. We even want the mommies to spank us. We want that kind of careful hurt.

From the mommies' phones, we erase the pictures of their real, long-lost daughters. The estranged, the deceased, the emotionally scarred. The daughters who followed careers to distant parts of the country, and those who pursued addictions down alleys and toilet bowls. Our boss pays extra when we agree to replace the lost daughter's photos with our own, so we upload pictures of our cake-smeared faces, T-ball game action shots, and our bodies naked, half submerged in bubble baths. For another cash bonus, we post pictures of the mommies on our social media accounts. We caption them *Best mom ever!* and *#blessed*. You never had a daughter named Jenny, we insist to one mother. Never a Sarah, and never a Claire. Those memories are simply the crossing wires of your aging minds. We're your only daughters. How could you forget?

Mommy Edith, it hurts, make it better! Mommy Roberta, tell us about the eighties! We don't feel good at all, Mommy Yolanda. Mommy Rhonda, how do we shave our legs?

More mothers, all the mothers, is what we tell the boss we want. We insist we're not in it only for paychecks. We don't talk about our expanding bank accounts, or how, after our shifts, we get manicures then meet at upscale bars and drink until we're warm. We eat takeout in bed while online splurging on designer denim, skin creams, and phones. Then we close our blackout curtains and take our sleeping pills. We hope that tonight, we'll get our eight hours. We hope that, before we return for our next shift, we'll get lucky and have sweet dreams of our own lost mothers extending their arms and welcoming all of us back.

As If in Prayer

My sister did not know what to do with her hands, or what to call her husband. He was three people, at least, and he ought to have had three names. He woke early, fed the dog, then hiked through the fog of the mountains. Once, he found and caught two ghosts in those woods, my sister's and his own, and carried them back to the house. He packed his ghost into his old pipe and, sitting on the wicker porch bench, smoked it into his body. By the time he was finished, my sister had joined him with her coffee. He packed the pipe once more, with her ghost, and placed it on her lap.

"You don't want any part of you left for annihilation time, not even your ghost," he said.

She trusted his predictions that the world would soon end, drew a deep puff, and exhaled slowly. *There are still things he does not know about me*, she thought. She made a crooked, closed-mouth smile he'd never seen before. He looked away toward the forest, then back at my sister. She seemed to him, as she smoked the pipe, as arresting and old as the mountains.

She cut wildflowers from the long grass surrounding the house, brought them in, and arranged them in vases for the windows. Each flower has a face, she thought, and anything with a face must have a ghost.

When she fell asleep, in the afternoon, she dreamt she had a batch of sons who fashioned weapons out of scrap wood planks and spare nails, then dragged her through the house. They dragged her outside, and, in the grass, beat her through the night. When they were finished, they carried her to the bathroom and took turns washing her wounds. When my sister woke, she felt as though her body had been hollowed and refilled.

My sister remembered going to the war as a young woman, where she was always surrounded by men. Some men gave her orders and some gave her ravenous glares. Some men she loved, and some she hated so fiercely she plotted their deaths. Then she was surrounded by only a single man who seemed to be in three places at once: the forest, the sky, and right in the house, where he waltzed her through the rooms. Their neighbors prepared for the end of the world in other ways than they did: They built bunkers, stocked water, filled cabinets with cans, put their hands together as if in prayer.

One night, my sister forgot to take her pills and could not sleep. She sat outside on the big, old porch, surrounded by cicadas and stars. She was the most alone she'd ever been. She was just as alone as you are now. She wanted to complete herself before the end, so she slid her hands under the skirt of her nightdress and thought of distant planets. That's where she went all by herself and didn't bring herself back.

My sister lost control of her hands, her husband, and her ghost. I lost track of my sister. Still, I imagine what comes next for us both is something better, something pristine. It's like she used to say to me when we were just little kids: Every tale in your bones can be loosed to the world. Anything you imagine may be so.

How to Love a Black Hole

Walk down the empty hall and stretch your arms towards the walls covered with canvases she painted to preserve candid scenes of your lives. Remember that invisibility is not absence. Feel for her everywhere. Check the chairs around the kitchen table, where she once made you laugh so hard that half-chewed meat hit the window. Slide apart her jackets and her dresses in the closet, and feel for her between soft, abandoned fabrics. Sit on the couch and try to intuit the force of her body, curled on the cushion beside you. Stream the sitcom you both liked to watch, where all turns out well for the scrappy couple by the end of every show.

Do not panic when items disappear. The wedding portraits can be reprinted, reframed. Her tubes of oil paint and her hair clips, the nicknacks she bought on your vacations are nothing but objects in the end. When your gifts of chocolates and flowers seem to vanish with vigor and speed, do not assume she is thankful for them or that they make her feel full. Don't replace the bottle of vodka when it disappears from the freezer. After a kitchen knife vanishes, vanish the others yourself. Buy a padlock strong enough to resist the force of her empty desire. Be calm but mindful and vigilant of the fact that in the end, she's mostly consuming herself.

Be calm but mindful and vigilant of her lightless mass, which enchants like a siren singing only for you. Don't believe her force conveys any honest emotion. As much as you feel you must stay close, leave the house. Order your cortado at the coffee shop and stay at the table by the window a little longer than usual. Even though you don't know the people around you, the way they chat in pairs, or do their laptop work, helps you feel a little less like you're floating in space. Meet Mark and Jerry for lunch. Let them tell you about their own recent quandaries: the asteroid that ripped through the house, an infestation of space debris that swirls no matter how much they clean. Pass through the park and watch children block one another's shots. At night, take a walk and, when you look at the stars, remember some of them are new.

If she stays in bed for eighteen-, twenty-four-, thirty-six-hour stretches, remind yourself that beds are not merely for the sick and tired, but they're also places for love. Arousal can be contagious, and you can try to inspire her to feel it too. Run your fingers over her body. Allow her obstinate gravity to pull them close, to circle and enter her mouth. Allow your appendages to be drawn into her and play make-believe. Pretending can sometimes turn into the real thing, so tell yourself that she is not lying underneath you, absorbing you with cold indifference. Pretend that if you love her fiercely enough, you will pull some light back out.

If she says, "I worry I'll devour your whole universe," lead her to the fire escape, show her the sun. Help her skin feel the mid-summer breeze, her ears hear the city. Help her smell the scent of lilacs and spot squirrels corkscrewing up trees. If she cries with her eyes closed, lick away her tears before they trickle back in through her mouth. Remind her that when a black hole and a star come close together the result, every time, is high-energy light. Though neither of you can see it now, it's there. Repeat it, it's there.

Acknowledgements

Thanks to the literary journals that published earlier versions of some of these stories. "Hear Me Out" in *Complete Sentence*, "When I Was Ten" in *Coffin Bell Journal*, "Miles," in *L'Esprit Literary Review*, "When We Shrunk" in *Peatsmoke Journal*, "Tornado Warnings" *in Bending Genres*, "High School Mixtape" in *The Nervous Breakdown*, "The Shamash" in *Ghost Parachute*, "As If in Prayer" in *Moon City Review*, and "Haunts" and "Go Back" in *SmokeLong Quarterly*.

About the Author

Rebecca Fishow is a fiction writer, painter, and educator. Her other books include *The Trouble With Language*, winner of the Holland Prize for Fiction, and the chapbook *The Opposite of Entropy*. She lives in Chicago with her husband and son. Find her at rebeccafishow.weebly.com.